First published 2021 by Laki Isra

Nusaybah – A Mermaid's Tale

Inspired by and dedicated to:

Maryah Isra Khan

&

Aamilah Isra Khan

- L.I.

This book belongs to

....

Age........

It was a beautiful day under the Ocean.

Nusaybah sat in front of the mirror
unable to decide which hair clip
Laura might like best,
and that made her worry.

She switched from pink to yellow,
until Mother called out,
'Nusaybah, you'll be late for school!'

'Going now,' she replied.

On her swim to mermaid school,
she hoped Laura would be
a little kinder today.

Laura was the most popular Mermaid in school. She wore beautifully sequinned dresses. Her long blonde hair flowed around her rosy cheeks.

Nusaybah did not dress or look like Laura, but she wanted Laura to like her.

Nusaybah signed into German class, sitting next to Laura, Meghan and Karina Mermaid.

'Laura, do you like my clip?'
Nusaybah asked.
'Whatever,' Laura replied.

The Mermaids began German class, which Nusaybah struggled with. Meghan helped her to pronounce some of the words – until Laura intervened.

'You work with me!'
Laura snapped at Meghan.

Before Nusaybah could utter a word, Laura had already sat in between her and Meghan.

'Laura, Meghan, Nusaybah!'
shouted Karina Mermaid,
swimming into class excitedly.

'The art group is starting again. Every
Friday after school.'

'That's fabulous,' declared Laura.

But Nusaybah's excitement about the art
group was short-lived; her heart sank
when she heard it would be on Friday.

In a whisper she asked, 'Can we ask
Miss Turtle to change it to another day?'

'No!' snapped Laura.

As disappointed as she was,
Nusaybah valued her Friday family
activity too much to give it up.

ART
CLUB

On her swim home from school with Mother, all Nusaybah could think about was how much fun the other mermaids would have at the art group without her.

'Are you okay?' Mother asked.

'I want to join the art group, but Laura won't agree to talk with Miss Turtle to change it.'

'Why?'

'You know how mean she is.'

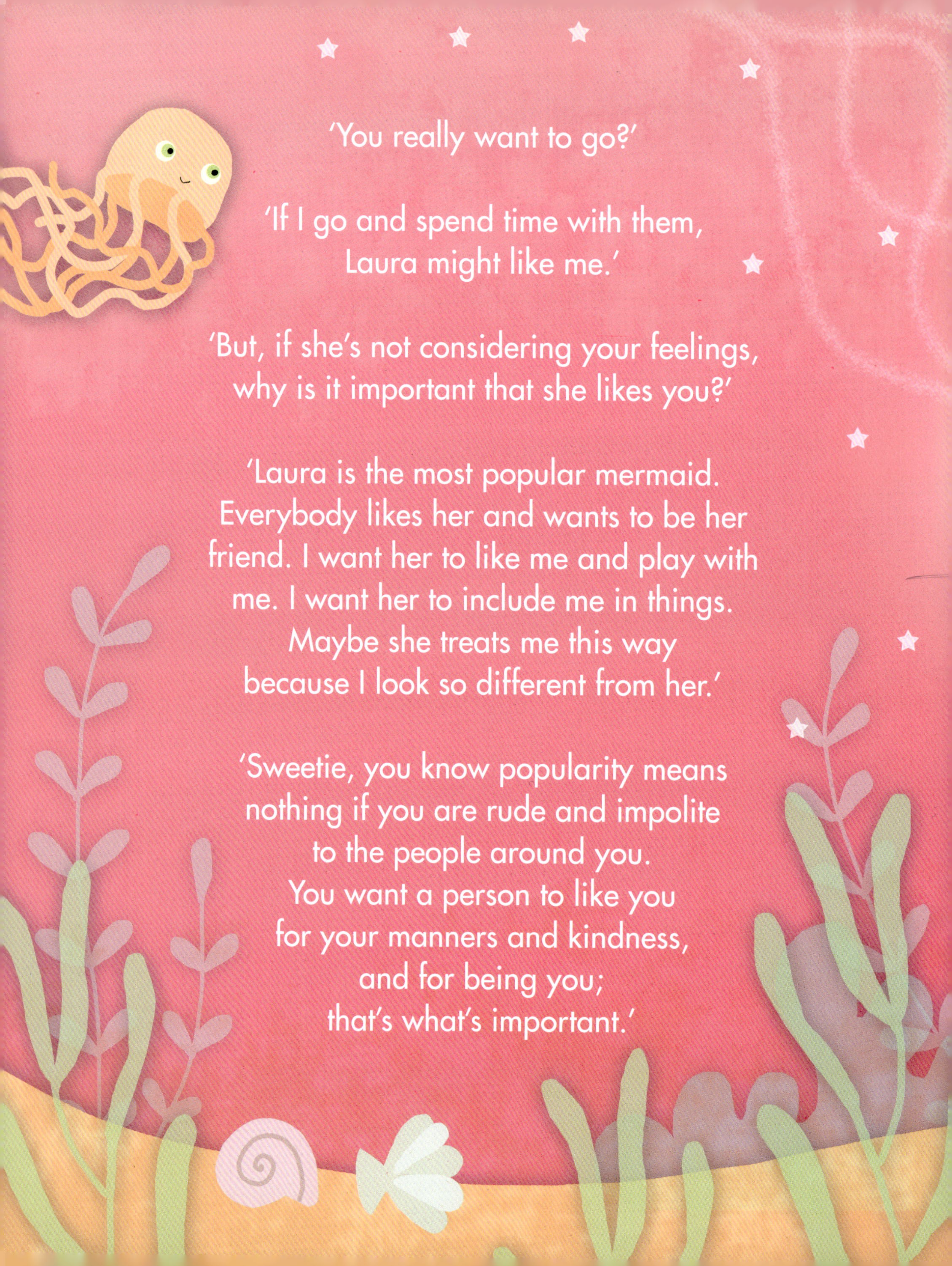

'You really want to go?'

'If I go and spend time with them,
Laura might like me.'

'But, if she's not considering your feelings,
why is it important that she likes you?'

'Laura is the most popular mermaid.
Everybody likes her and wants to be her
friend. I want her to like me and play with
me. I want her to include me in things.
Maybe she treats me this way
because I look so different from her.'

'Sweetie, you know popularity means
nothing if you are rude and impolite
to the people around you.
You want a person to like you
for your manners and kindness,
and for being you;
that's what's important.'

Mother's words did not comfort Nusaybah.

Then Mother told her about the surprise waiting for her at home.

Gradually Nusaybah's frown disappeared and she swam faster.

Once home, Mother presented a wrapped gift to her daughter.

Nusaybah unwrapped a purple sparkly book.

'It's from Nan, and she has written out lots of new words for you to learn and spell for Friday.'

'I love it!'

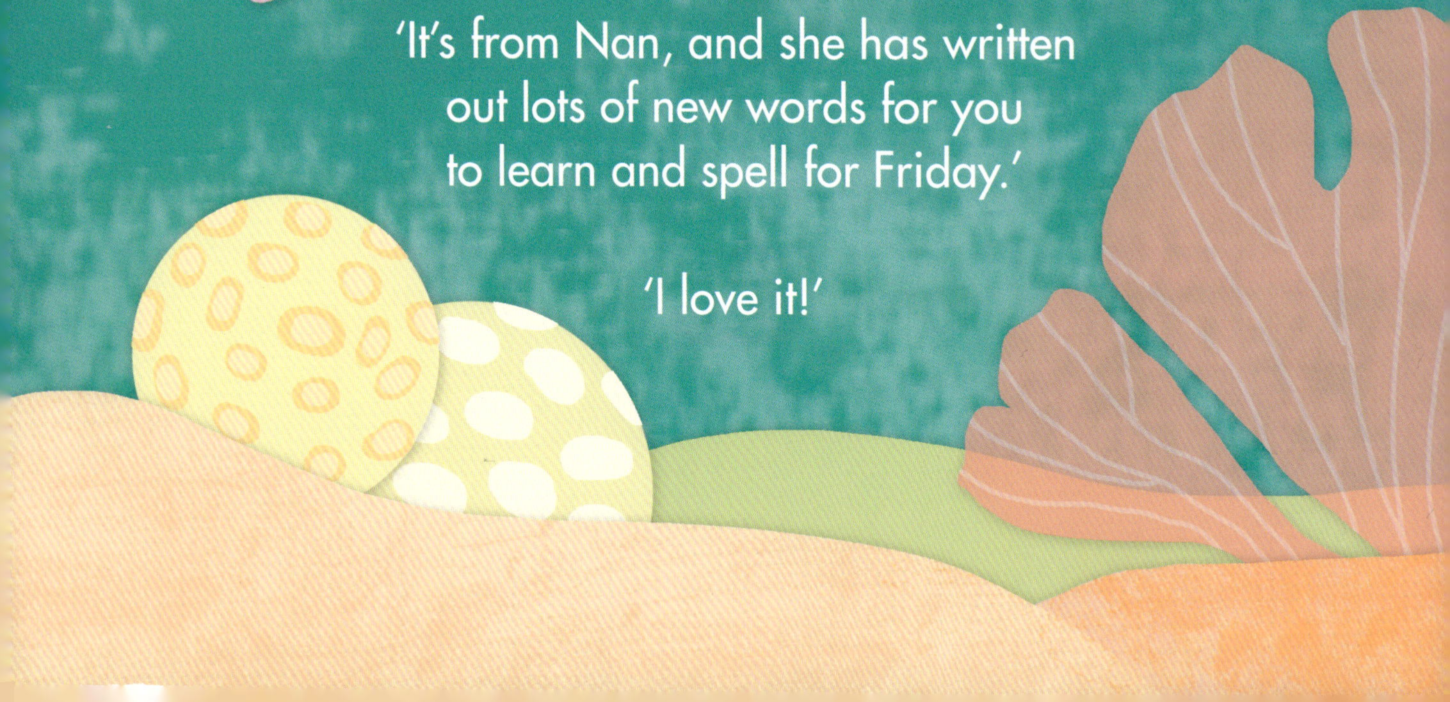

It was the morning of the
Annual Squiggle Contest;
Nusaybah woke up with
a fluttering inside her belly.

It made her feel funny.

The Squiggle Contest
was a big thing,
and Nusaybah had
looked forward to it.

But now she was worried.

How would she do today?

Would Laura be mean to her
again if she didn't do well?

Nusaybah swam into the contest hall, and took her place beside the other mermaids who were already seated.

'It's time to begin,' said Dugong Den.

'Now, there is a little twist to this squiggle contest.

You must think of 10 words to write.

But as you are all learning a second language, you must write the words both in English and another language.

Good luck everybody!'

ANNUAL
SQUIGGLE CON
JUDGE

Nusaybah became nervous.
She was not good in German!

All the words she'd practised with
Meghan had vanished from her mind.

She chewed her lip and tapped
her pencil to her head.
Think, she told herself, think.

Then, in a flash, it came to her!

'Does the second language have to be
the one we're learning in school?'
she asked excitedly.

Laura shot her a confused look.

'No,' replied Dugong Den.
'Any language is fine.'

Nusaybah felt relieved.
She quickly got to writing!

When the contest ended,
the judges spoke with each other
while the mermaids waited eagerly.

'We have come to a decision,'
announced Dugong Den.

'This year's squiggle contest
has been splendid.
Well done, everybody.
Now, the winner has done
exceptionally well, writing 11 words
in both English and Arabic.
The winner is adorable Nusaybah!'

Dugong Den presented Nusaybah
with a beautiful trophy that read
Squiggle Contest Winner.

Squiggle Contest Winner
CO…
…ST JUDGE

All the mermaids began to murmur,
and some asked, 'What is Arabic?'

Nusaybah sat up tall, her smile wide.

Nusaybah's friends ran up
to congratulate her.

'You won the squiggle contest!'
squealed Karina.

'Nusaybah, you won!' exclaimed Meghan.

'Will you work with me and Karina on
the languages project next week?'

'Of course.'

'Yay!' said Meghan.

Everybody clapped as Nusaybah
held the trophy and had
her photo taken with the judges.

Later that day, the other Mermaids
asked how she had learnt Arabic.

Nusaybah proudly told them
all about how she attended
Arabic classes with her
family on Fridays.

Her friends were delighted that
Nusaybah was so good at a language
they had not even heard of.

They all crowded around her,
congratulating her,
and looking at her in admiration.

Nusaybah's heart filled with joy.

It had been a wonderful day and she
swam home wearing a gigantic smile.

Squiggle
Contest
Winner

The next morning Nusaybah woke up feeling elated.

She swam up to Mermaid school, and was greeted by Dugong Den, Miss Turtle, Seahorse Sam, Meghan Mermaid, Karina Mermaid, and the jellyfish.

The best thing was that her friends, Meghan and Karina, had spoken to Miss Turtle and changed the day of the art group. Nusaybah was delighted.

Now she could make art with her friends without missing her Arabic class.

And she no longer cared that Laura didn't want to be her friend. She had real friends who liked her for who she was.

SPOT THE DIFFERENCES IN THE FISH!
THEN ADD MORE TO THE SCENE,
AND COLOR IT AS YOU LIKE.

Things that make me unique

What qualities should a good friend have?

Draw a picture of
you and your friend!

Sea creatures are wonderful!

Can you research these animals and then draw them?

Sea horse

Crab

Octopus

Shells

Sea turtle

Jellyfish

Draw or write about your most favourite sea creature.